TEAMWORK WORKS

BOOK SERIES

Published By

OHC Group LLC
PO Box 7839, Westlake Village, CA 91359

SECOND EDITION
ISBN 0-9763213-3-5

Printed and bound in China

The Only Hearts Girls™ formed
The Only Hearts Club® in a bond
of true friendship. They are a fun-
loving bunch of friends who are
always there for one another. They
laugh, share secrets and have the
greatest adventures together. Most
importantly, they encourage one
another to think with their hearts
and to try and do the right thing.

Contents

Briana's Ready to be a Soccer Star

It was early on Saturday morning, but Briana Joy was already up and running around the house. She was so excited! After all the waiting, soccer season was finally here, and her friends from the Only Hearts Club were going to be on her team again! They were a fun-loving group of six girls who were always there for one another. They laughed, shared secrets and had the greatest adventures together. Most importantly, they followed their hearts and always tried to do the right thing – even though it wasn't always easy. Briana and her friends were a year older, so they'd be playing in the league for the big girls!

Briana had been preparing for this day for months. She had practiced soccer all summer with her big sister, Alex. She had made her dad go outside after dinner most nights to kick the ball with her until it got dark. Even Briana's little dachshund, Longfellow, tried to play soccer with her, barking and chasing after the soccer ball, which looked twice as big as him! Best of all, she had even convinced her parents to let her take lessons from Ms. Webb, the girls' soccer coach at the local high school. Briana was ready to be a superstar!

Finders Keepers?

Briana's mom drove her to the team's first practice at the school field and dropped her off. "Have fun!" her mom said as Briana bounded from the car, her curly brown hair bouncing off her shoulders.

Briana stopped and looked back. "Oh, Mom," she said. "We're not little kids; we're big girls now. This isn't about running around and just having fun anymore. It's about playing well and winning."

Her mom nodded. "OK," she said. "But don't forget how much fun you had with soccer last year."

Briana waved goodbye and turned to run to the field. She rolled her eyes as she moved away from the car. *Ugh,* she thought, *last year? Who cares about last year? It was fun, but so what?* To Briana, they had been like babies last year. All they did was run around the field laughing and yelling and kicking the ball this way and that, and they lost as many games as they won. That wasn't real soccer. *This year will be different*, she promised herself.

She was wearing her brand new white soccer cleats. Not only would she play like a star this year, she'd look like one, too. Briana smiled as she reached the field, where her friends from the Only Hearts Club, Anna Sophia, Karina Grace, Olivia Hope, Taylor Angelique and Lily Rose, were chasing each other in a game of tag.

Within minutes, everyone had arrived, and Coach Andrew called the girls together. "OK, everyone," he said. "Welcome to soccer season!" The girls clapped their hands excitedly. "Our first order of business will be handing out uniforms and picking a team name." The circle of girls buzzed with anticipation. "I picked up our uniforms yesterday afternoon," said Coach Andrew as he reached into a duffel bag, "and our team color is...TURQUOISE BLUE!" He pulled out a pile of uniforms – bright turquoise blue shorts and warm-up jackets, pretty yellow jerseys with dark blue numbers and light blue stripes. The girls jumped up and down and cheered. These uniforms were cool!

"Now, instead of handing out the uniforms myself,

I'm going to let you girls pick them," said Coach Andrew. "Maybe people will want to wear the same number they had last year."

The girls started looking through the pile of uniforms. Everyone took the same number as last year – everyone, that is, except Briana. Briana had worn number 2 last year, but she wasn't looking for number 2 this year. She had decided over the summer that since she was going to be the best player on the team, she'd wear number 1. But Anna had worn number 1 last year, and she was looking for it in the pile of uniforms when Briana spotted it and grabbed it. "Yes!" Briana exclaimed. "Number 1 for the superstar!"

Anna laughed and walked over to Briana. She thought Briana was teasing her by taking her number 1 uniform. "Ha ha," said Anna as she put out her hand. "OK, Briana, hand it over."

"What? Why?" said Briana as she held the uniform behind her back, away from Anna. "I want number 1 this year. Finders keepers."

"What, are you kidding me?" asked Anna, sounding surprised. "Everyone took their same number from last year, except you. Can I please have my number 1?"

"Nope," said Briana. "Ms. Webb was number 1 when she played soccer in college, and she was a superstar. If I'm going to be a superstar this year, then I have to have a superstar number. You can just have my old number 2."

Anna shook her head and walked slowly to the one uniform left on the ground – number 2. She picked it up sadly and held it under her arm. All the girls stared at Briana, but no one said anything.

"OK, now it's time to choose our team name," said Coach Andrew over the girls' excited chatter. "Let's have some suggestions."

The girls started calling out ideas. "The Blue Rockets," said one. "The Bluebirds," said another. "The Blue Monsters," giggled another, and everybody laughed.

Last year their uniforms had been purple, and they had named their team The Purple Popsicles. The girls, including Briana, thought that was a funny name at the time, but now Briana didn't like it. *What a silly name for a soccer team,* she thought to herself. *We need a really cool name this year, a name that a real soccer team would have – like the Stars!*

"How about the Stars?" said Briana, but nobody seemed to hear her. They were too busy shouting out funny names.

"Hey, how about the Blue Buffaloes?" shouted Olivia. Everyone laughed again.

"I know, we should be the Blue Ballerinas!" said Karina.

"Yes! Yes! The Blue Ballerinas!" the girls chanted.

"All right," said Coach Andrew. "It sounds like our team name is The Blue Ballerinas!"

"Hooray!" cheered the girls. They were all jumping up and down...except Briana.

Briana couldn't believe it. *What are my friends doing?* she wondered. Briana crossed her arms and made a face. *Well,* she thought to herself, *if my friends aren't going to act like real soccer players, then I'm going to make sure we act like a real soccer team!*

Practice Makes Perfect

After just a few practices, it was clear that Briana was the best player on the team. She was very good at dribbling and controlling the ball, and when she took a shot, the ball came off her foot like a rocket. When Coach Andrew split up the team to scrimmage at the end of each practice, Briana's side always won, and she scored almost all her team's goals.

But Briana was getting a little frustrated about the way practice had been going. Coach Andrew didn't coach the way Ms. Webb had coached her privately during summer. Briana felt as though she didn't get as much attention from Coach Andrew. And she didn't get to do as much of the fun stuff she'd done with Ms. Webb, like shooting at the goal and doing tricks with the ball. Briana wished Coach Andrew would coach like Ms. Webb. Maybe Briana could help make him coach more that way, or at least show her teammates the "fun" way to practice. She decided it was time to liven up practice.

At the next practice, when Coach Andrew asked the girls to pair up and pass the ball back and forth, Briana went off on her own and took shots at the goal. When Coach Andrew asked the girls to dribble the ball back and forth through the orange cones he had placed on the ground, Briana shot the ball at the cones and tried to knock them down. And when he had the girls work on their throw-ins, Briana did tricks with the soccer ball, trying to bounce it from her foot to her knee and then back to her foot.

As practice ended, Coach Andrew thanked the girls for their hard work and reminded them that they had their first game on Saturday morning. He also asked Briana if she could stay after practice so he could talk to her for a minute.

After the other girls had left practice, Coach Andrew sat down with her. "Briana, you are clearly very talented and very good at soccer," he said. "But sometimes you don't seem interested in following my instructions, and you're starting to distract your teammates from practice as well. What's going on?"

"We do such boring things at practice – dribbling

and passing and stuff," she said. "And you make us do it over and over and over. I already know how to do all that. I just want to do some fun stuff and practice things that will make me a superstar."

"Well," began Coach Andrew, "maybe you've noticed that some of your teammates aren't quite as good at dribbling and passing as you are. If we want to be a good team and have fun this year, all of us need to be good at the basics. That's why I have you girls work on them every week. I'd appreciate it if you could follow instructions and set a good example for your teammates."

"OK," said Briana. "See you at the game on Saturday, Coach." But Briana was not convinced. Just because her teammates weren't very good at soccer, was she going to have to spend the whole season doing these boring practice drills? Ugh. Why couldn't they just try harder or be better at soccer like her? *Who cares about practice anyway,* she thought as she walked to her dad's car. *The games are what really matter.* She'd show everyone what a real soccer player looked like on Saturday.

Briana Wins, but Loses

It was Saturday morning, time for Briana's first game of the season! She was so excited! She made sure her mom and dad got her to the game extra early.

They were playing against a team called the Green Frogs. Briana started at center forward. The referee blew his whistle and the game was on! Briana was the best player on the field. She was great on defense, often taking the ball away from the other team, and she was equally good on offense, dribbling the ball through the Green Frogs' defense. Before long, she had scored three goals, and by halftime the Blue Ballerinas were winning 3 to 0.

The parents were all clapping for the girls as they came off the field at halftime. "Great first half, Briana!" several people called out. "Way to go!" Briana had definitely been the star.

"Good job!" said Coach Andrew to the girls as they

drank juice and ate orange slices that Lily's mom had brought to the game. "Let's keep it up in the second half!"

Before they went back onto the field, Coach Andrew took Briana aside. "Briana, you played a great first half," he said. "It seems we're a better team than the Green Frogs, and it looks like we're going to win this game. In the second half I'd like you to work on getting your teammates involved. Concentrate on passing the ball and see if we can get some of the other girls to score goals, too. It's important that your teammates improve so we get better as a team, and that everyone participates and has fun."

"OK," Briana nodded.

Soon after the second half began, Briana was dribbling the ball down the field. As she got close to the goal, she saw Anna standing alone at the other side of the goal, waving her hands and calling for the ball. Briana remembered what Coach Andrew had said about passing, so instead of shooting the ball, Briana sent a perfect pass to Anna. All Anna had to do was shoot it into the goal. But she missed the ball! It rolled over her foot and out of bounds!

Anna was embarrassed. She hung her head and stared at the ground.

"That's OK, Anna!" said Coach Andrew from the sideline as he clapped his hands. "Good try!" The parents shouted out encouraging words as well.

Olivia ran over and patted Anna on the back. "Don't worry," Olivia said. "You'll get it next time."

Briana watched from the other side of the field. *That was a perfect pass,* she thought to herself. *How could Anna have missed that easy goal? If my teammates are going to mess up, then I can't trust them. I'm not passing the ball to them anymore.*

Before long, the Green Frogs figured out how to stop the Ballerinas. They had two or three players guard Briana every time she got the ball. Since she wouldn't pass, the Green Frogs would eventually take the ball away from her every time.

"Pass it, Briana, pass it!" Coach Andrew called from the sideline. But Briana didn't listen.

Soon, the Green Frogs had scored three goals of their own and the game was tied 3 to 3.

As the game was about to end, Taylor had the ball

and was dribbling toward the goal. She saw that Anna was open near the goal again. She passed it to her. This time, Anna stopped the ball nicely and was about to shoot it into the goal. But just as she lifted her leg to kick the ball, someone crashed into her, knocked her down and took the ball away. But it wasn't one of the players from the Green Frogs. It was Briana! Briana quickly controlled the ball and fired it into the goal just as time ran out.

Briana threw her arms into the air. "Yes!" she cried, jumping up and down. "My fourth goal, my fourth goal!"

But this time, no one else was cheering with her. All eyes were on Anna, who was lying on the ground. Coach Andrew and Anna's parents ran onto the field.

Taylor, Olivia, Lily, Karina and the other girls crowded around Anna as Coach Andrew and her parents helped her up.

"Anna! Anna! Are you OK?" Taylor asked.

Anna nodded her head yes. They could see that she was crying.

"Are you hurt?" Lily asked.

Anna shook her head no.

After a few minutes, her father said, "Anna seems fine. I think the only things that may be hurt are some feelings."

While Coach Andrew continued checking Anna, the other girls turned and walked over to Briana, who was still standing on the other side of the field.

"What was that all about?" Karina asked Briana.

"That wasn't very nice," said Olivia.

Briana had a funny feeling in her heart, but she ignored it. "What?" asked Briana. "I didn't want Anna to mess up again. I wanted to make sure we won. We won, right? So what's the problem?"

"It's not just about winning, Briana," said Taylor. "Look around. Does our team look happy because we won? Do the parents look happy? Does Coach Andrew look happy? I don't think so."

Briana looked around. Taylor was right. Most of the girls on the team were still huddled around Anna, trying to make sure she was OK. Anna was still upset. None of the parents were cheering. And Coach Andrew certainly didn't look very happy.

"Briana, last year we all worked together and had a lot of fun playing soccer," said Lily. "But this year it seems like you're only interested in yourself and in winning."

"Well," Briana started, "I tried to give the ball to Anna earlier in the game and she messed up. I didn't want that to happen again, so the next time I made sure I had the ball. You guys just aren't as good as me at soccer. You all need to practice more and try harder so you can be more like me and we can win."

Briana was confused. She had just scored to win the game, but she didn't feel good inside. In fact, she felt terrible. Something wasn't right, but what?

Taylor shook her head as Briana turned away and walked toward her parents. "What happened to nice, sweet Briana?" she asked in a quiet voice.

"I think she's acting more like a Blue Monster than a Blue Ballerina," said Olivia, and they smiled.

Family Time

T hat night after dinner, Briana's family gathered in the family room to talk about the past week and what had happened in their lives during that time. Briana settled into the big plaid club chair that she liked so much. It was just the right size for an adult – or for two little girls. Whenever one of the Only Hearts Club members came over for a sleepover, Briana and her friend would sit together in the club chair to watch a movie before bedtime.

Briana's dad spoke first. He was an architect, and he gave the family an update about the exciting project he was working on in his spare time for free – designing the new community center for their town. Briana's mom was a lawyer. She told the family about an important legal case that she had just finished working on for a client.

Then it was the children's turn. Briana's big sister, Alex, told the family about junior high school and how her sixth-grade soccer team was so much fun and was doing so well. Briana was proud of her sister. Someday she knew she would go to the same school and, hopefully, play soccer there just like Alex. Briana's little brother, Carter, was only two years old. He was too little to say much. He sat in his high chair, eating carrots and laughing a lot. Then it was Briana's turn.

"As you all know, I scored all our goals in the game today," Briana bragged. "I was the best player on the field. I won the game for our team. I was a superstar."

"My, there certainly are a lot of 'I's' in your story," said her dad. "I seem to remember there were some other girls out there on the field with you, too, weren't there?"

"Daaa-aaad," Briana said, rolling her eyes. She knew he was teasing her with that question. "Of course there were other players on the field with me. They just weren't very good."

"Well, do you think you were a good teammate?" her father asked. "Did you do your best to help your team?"

"Um, I dunno," fibbed Briana. "I mean, I tried passing to Anna once, but she messed it up, so after that I decided I'd just do it myself."

"So you gave your teammates only one chance?" asked her mom. "That doesn't sound very helpful. What do we do in our family when you're trying to learn something new or improve on something?"

"What do you mean?" asked Briana.

"For example, do you remember when you were trying to learn how to tie your shoes when you were little?" asked her mom.

"Um, sort of," said Briana.

"Well, you didn't know how to do it at first, and then you slowly learned how. When you were learning, it took you a very long time to tie your shoes by yourself," her mom recalled with a smile.

"Oh, I remember," said her sister with a laugh. "You were sooooo slowwwww at tying your shoes. We'd all be ready to go out, and you'd take ten minutes to tie your little shoes. It took us forever to get out of the house. I just wanted mom and dad to tie your shoes for you so we could leave already."

"But did we tie your shoes, or let you do it?" asked her mom.

"You let me try, and pretty soon I learned how to do it just fine!" said Briana, giving her sister a look.

"You were so proud!" her father remembered. "Do you know why we did that?"

"So I could learn how to do it myself?" asked Briana.

"Right," said her dad with a smile. "Practice makes perfect. You should try to give your teammates a chance and see what they can do. You might be surprised."

That night as she got ready for bed, Briana thought about her family's after-dinner discussion. She still wasn't convinced. Tying your shoes was one thing, but soccer was something entirely different. As she sat on the floor and scratched Longfellow behind his ears, she thought about what had happened at the game, and felt that heaviness in her heart again. But why? She had single-handedly won the game for her team, but as she climbed into bed, she had a sad feeling in her heart.

A Sudden Twist for Briana

The Blue Ballerinas' next game, against the Red Rockets, started out much as the previous one had. Once Briana got the ball, no one on the other team could get it away from her. She scored the first goal, and then another goal, and it wasn't even halftime yet. Meanwhile, her teammates were getting more and more frustrated because she wasn't sharing the ball or being a team player. After the second goal, none of her teammates even came over to congratulate her. Briana didn't notice. She was too busy being a superstar.

As the game went on, Coach Andrew noticed that when Briana had the ball, some of her teammates stopped running. He realized they were starting to give up on Briana. They thought she would never pass the ball to them, so why should they even try?

"Briana," Coach Andrew called out, "let's work on passing the ball a little bit."

His comment went in one ear and out the other. Briana was determined to win the game by herself again.

Soon Briana had the ball again and was dribbling through the defense toward the goal. She was about to score, but just as she prepared to shoot the ball, she slipped on a wet spot on the field and fell down.

"Owwwww!" Briana cried as she fell, clutching her left ankle.

Coach Andrew and Briana's dad rushed onto the field.

"Briana, Briana! Are you OK?" asked her dad.

"My ankle! My ankle!" Briana cried. "I think I broke my ankle!"

A hush fell over the field as Coach Andrew examined Briana's ankle.

"I don't think it's broken," the coach said. "I think it's just sprained."

Briana's dad carried her to the sideline.

"We should probably go to the hospital to have that checked out," he said.

"No, I feel a little better," said Briana. "Can I just

stay and watch the rest of the game?"

After consulting with Coach Andrew, her dad agreed. They sat Briana on a bench, propped up her ankle, and put a big bag of ice on it.

All the girls on the team crowded around Briana on the sideline. "Are you OK?" they asked her, one after another.

Before they went back onto the field, each of the Only Hearts Club girls gave her a hug, even Anna, to whom Briana had not yet apologized for stealing the ball in the first game. Briana felt a lump in her throat. And it wasn't because her ankle hurt. She wondered why everyone was being so nice to her. She certainly hadn't been very nice to them recently.

"Let's win one for Briana!" cheered Taylor, and the Blue Ballerinas ran back onto the field.

Soon the game resumed – without Briana. At first the Blue Ballerinas were a team in disarray. They appeared lost without Briana, and before long the Red Rockets had the upper hand. They scored a couple of quick goals before halftime to tie the score at 2 to 2.

At halftime, Coach Andrew encouraged the team.

"OK girls," he said, "Briana's hurt and can't help us for the rest of this game. We need everyone to step up and play as a team if we want to have a chance. Believe in each other and trust each other. And most of all, go out there and have fun."

Briana Listens to Her Heart

Things started to change in the second half. The Blue Ballerinas started using teamwork to stop the Red Rockets and move the ball toward their goal. They were helping each other on defense. When they had the ball, they passed it around and tried to get it to whomever was open near the goal so she could shoot. Before long, Olivia made a nice pass to Taylor, who scored a goal. The Red Rockets scored the next two goals to go ahead 4 to 3, but the Blue Ballerinas continued to play well. The next time the Blue Ballerinas got the ball, Lily and Karina dribbled and passed the ball back and forth until they got right in front of the Red Rockets' goal. Karina took a shot and tied the score 4 to 4. The Blue Ballerinas all ran together and jumped up and down while hugging Karina and Lily.

"Whooo-eee! Go, Ballerinas, go!" yelled the girls as they clapped and laughed.

Olivia ran by the sideline and yelled to Coach Andrew, "Now this is fun!"

Briana watched all this quietly from the sideline. *What's happening?* she wondered to herself. They weren't winning the game, but they sure were having a good time. Everyone seemed so happy and excited. She smiled to herself as her thoughts drifted back to the year before. This is what it had been like all last season. The Only Hearts Club girls had played together as a team and had laughed and had fun at every game.

Briana realized she missed being on the field, not just because she missed playing soccer, but because she missed having fun with her best friends. Now Briana knew why she'd had that funny feeling in her heart. It was because she was being selfish and she wasn't being a good friend to her fellow Only Hearts Club members or her other teammates. Briana knew it was time to listen to her heart and try to do the right thing.

She got up off the bench and hobbled over to the sideline so she could get a better view of the action. In her heart, Briana found herself believing in her teammates and rooting for them. A little voice inside

her was saying, "Go, Taylor! Go, Lily! Go, Karina! Go, Olivia! Go, Anna!" Soon, she was cheering out loud with the parents who were standing next to her.

"Go, Blue Ballerinas! You can do it!" she called. "Come on guys, we can win this game!"

As time was winding down, Taylor got the ball. She started to dribble but then looked up and saw Anna standing all alone near the goal, just as she had been in the first game, when Briana passed her the ball and Anna missed it. All the girls knew that Anna felt bad about that experience, and that she had been practicing extra hard since then to make sure it didn't happen again. As two Red Rockets players converged on Taylor, she passed the ball to Anna without hesitating. Anna stopped the ball, and in one quick motion kicked it into the goal!

The Blue Ballerinas had won!

All the girls rushed over to Anna and gave her a big group hug as they jumped up and down with excitement. Anna was smiling from ear to ear.

"Hooray for Anna! Hooray for Taylor! Go, Blue Ballerinas!" their teammates cheered. Everyone was smiling and laughing, including Coach Andrew and all the parents.

Briana was happy for her teammates, but she felt a little left out, standing alone on the sideline while the girls romped around the field.

Then Taylor turned toward Briana and said in a loud voice, "Hey, this was a team victory, and we have one more teammate we haven't congratulated yet!"

The girls ran over to Briana and crowded around her. "Hooray for Briana!" Taylor cheered. "Briana scored our first two goals and helped us win, too!"

Briana appreciated the compliment, but she knew there were some things she had to say. "Thanks, guys," she began. "You played a great game, and I'm happy we won. But even more importantly, watching you made me realize why I really like soccer – because we all get to be with each other and have fun together!"

The girls hugged Briana and started to pick up their things to go home.

"Wait," said Briana. "There's just one more thing."

The girls looked at her. "What is it?" asked Lily.

"Well, my heart's been telling me something for

a few days now, and I finally realized what it's been saying," Briana said. Then she slowly pulled her number 1 jersey over her head, leaving her in her undershirt.

"This number belongs to someone else," said Briana, holding up the shirt. "Someone who was our superstar today, and someone I'm proud to have as a teammate."

She limped slowly over to Anna and handed her the number 1 jersey. "From my heart to yours," Briana said.

♡ Only Hearts Club™ ♡

Read all the Only Hearts Girls' heartwarming storybooks.

It's Hard To Say Good-Bye
When her friend loses her dog, Taylor Angelique finds a new puppy for her. But will Taylor Angelique keep the cute little puppy for herself?

Horse Sense
Olivia Hope's horse develops a slight limp right before the big show. Will she go for the blue ribbon or choose to save her horse?

Dancing Dilemma
Karina Grace is the best dancer in school. Will she let her talent get in the way of her friendships?

Teamwork Works
Briana Joy is a superstar on the soccer field. Will she try to win the game by herself or be a good teammate and help a friend?

Two Smart Cookies
Anna Sophia's pie is ruined just hours before the big bake-off. Can she whip up Grandma's secret recipe in time?

Peep for Keeps
Lily Rose discovers a lost baby bird in the forest. Should she keep it as a pet or return it to nature?